MOJANG
MINECRAFT

OFFICIAL
THE NETHER & THE END
STICKER BOOK

By Stephanie Milton
Illustrated by Ryan Marsh
Designed by Joe Bolder and Ryan Gale

Special thanks to Alex Wiltshire, Jennifer Hammervald, Amanda Ström, and Filip Thoms

RANDOM HOUSE NEW YORK

© 2018 Mojang AB and Mojang Synergies AB.
MINECRAFT and MOJANG are trademarks or registered trademarks of Mojang Synergies AB. All rights reserved.
Published in the United States by Random House Children's Books, a division of Penguin Random House LLC, 1745 Broadway,
New York, NY 10019, and in Canada by Penguin Random House Canada Limited, Toronto. Originally published in the United Kingdom by
Egmont Publishing UK, London, in 2018. Random House and the colophon are registered trademarks of Penguin Random House LLC.
rhcbooks.com
minecraft.net
ISBN 978-0-593-12469-7
MANUFACTURED IN CHINA
10 9 8 7
First Random House Edition 2020

NETHER EQUIPMENT

SURVIVAL
WITH BEAR

Psst! I hear you're thinking about visiting the Nether?
Listen closely—you're going to need all the help you can get.

A true survivor always has the right equipment for the job.
Find some armor to wear, then craft some items to protect yourself.

DIAMOND SWORD RECIPE

SHIELD RECIPE

NETHER PORTAL

Oh hey! Do you need some help building a Nether portal?
I just love building!

Find some obsidian block stickers on your sticker sheet, then
finish constructing the Nether portal.

BUILDING
WITH SPARKS

NETHER PORTAL

Nether portals allow you to travel from
the Overworld to the Nether. You'll need
at least 10 blocks of obsidian to build one
and it must be at least 4 x 5 blocks in size,
but you can leave the corners out. Once
the portal is built, activate it with a flint
and steel, then step through.

NETHER MOBS

COMBAT
WITH SCOUT

If you're looking for advice about how to deal with the Nether's mobs, you've come to the right person—I've faced these monsters many times and lived to tell the tale.

Find the sticker for each mob info card to learn all about them.

ZOMBIE PIGMAN

Hostility	5	Health	20
Attack	13	XP	5
Drops			

ℹ Pick off zombie pigmen one by one to avoid being swarmed.

ENDERMAN

Hostility	5	Health	40
Attack	10	XP	5
Drops			

ℹ Endermen are rare in the Nether. Wear a pumpkin to prevent hostility.

MAGMA CUBE

Hostility	7	Health	16
Attack	6	XP	4
Drops			

ℹ There are 3 sizes of magma cube—only big and small ones drop magma cream.

BLAZE

Hostility	10	Health	20
Attack	9	XP	10
Drops			

ℹ Blazes spawn in Nether fortresses, shoot fireballs, and are damaged by snowballs.

FISHING ROD RECIPE

GHAST

Hostility	10	Health	10
Attack	25	XP	5
Drops			

Ghasts are fierce foes. Reel one in with a fishing rod, then attack it with a sword.

SKELETON

Hostility	7	Health	20
Attack	5	XP	5
Drops			

Skeletons are a common mob but only occasionally pop up in Nether fortresses.

WITHER SKELETON

Hostility	9	Health	20
Attack	10	XP	5
Drops			

Wither skeletons drop their skulls, which they need to summon the wither boss mob.

SNOWBALLS

Snowballs can be obtained when you break a snow block with a shovel.

A TERRIBLE FORTRESS

Good day! Care to explore this magnificent fortress with me?
No doubt there'll be some wonderful discoveries waiting for us inside!

Navigate the maze to find the exit, picking up loot as you go.
Do try to avoid the mobs, though—they don't look very friendly. . . .

GOLDEN CHESTPLATE

DIAMOND HORSE ARMOR

START

GOLDEN SWORD

IRON HORSE ARMOR

FINISH

SADDLE

OBSIDIAN

NETHER WART

7

GHASTLY ENCOUNTER

You're crossing the Nether terrain when you hear a terrifying shriek. You look up and see a ghast. It may be the Nether's most dangerous mob, but if you keep calm and use your head, you can escape in one piece.

Use stickers from your sticker sheet to complete the story.

The wailing is getting louder. You look up and see a

[ ] floating in the air above you. In a panic you

begin to run, but there's nowhere to go. You shoot an

[ ] at the monsters, but you miss. The ghast opens

its mouth and a [ ] comes hurtling toward you.

You dive out of the way just in time, then search your

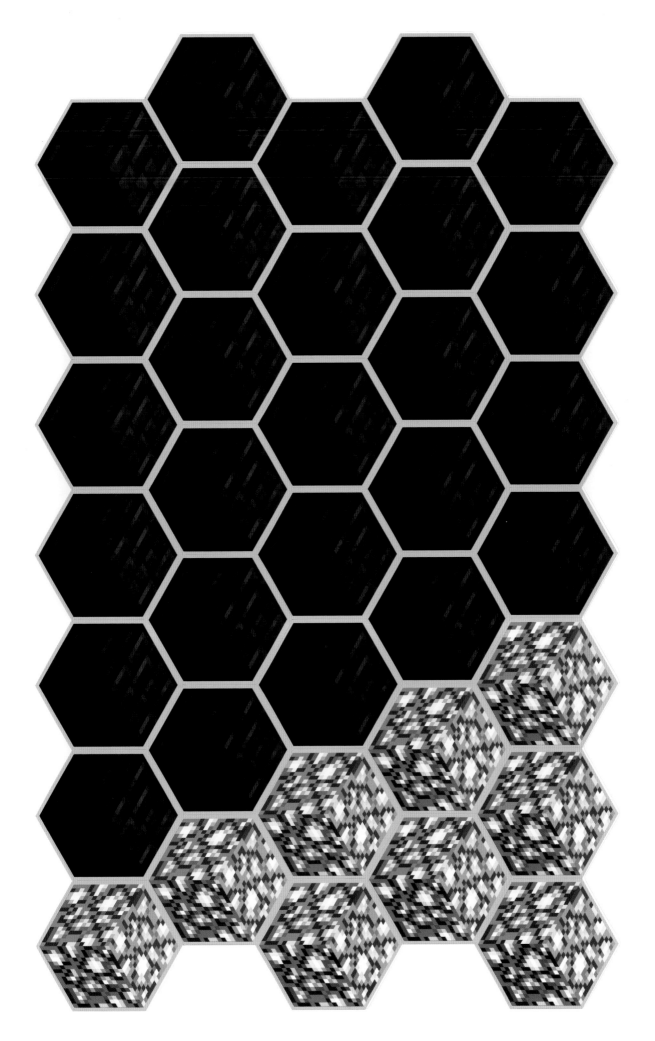

inventory to find some ⬚ blocks and quickly build an emergency shelter. This gives you a few minutes to make a plan. You don't have much equipment, but you head back outside. In desperation you use your ⬚ to reel the ghast toward you, then finish it off with your ⬚. Victory is yours! You see a ⬚ drop from the ghast as you finish it off. Unfortunately it falls into some ⬚ and is lost forever. Lesson learned—next time you fight a ghast, you'll make sure you defeat it over solid ground.

TAKING SHELTER

*Isn't being in the Nether super fun? It's so orange and burny!
It can't hurt to find somewhere to take shelter, though, just in case
you find yourself in a spot of trouble. . . .*

Let's repair and seal off a section of the fortress with Nether brick.
And while you're in there, why not light it up with glowstone?

11

NETHER LOOT

Now that you're safely back in the Overworld, you can take a proper look at all the Nether loot you collected and discover what it can be used for. I just love new crafting recipes!

Read the clue next to each item, then find the correct sticker for the box.

1

This substance burns forever, so it's really useful if you want to make a fireplace for your home. Just make sure it's not near any flammable blocks!

2

Light sources can be crafted from this item. It can also be used to make spectral arrows, which outline your targets so you can keep track of them.

3

This spooky-looking block is handy for making traps. Players and mobs will sink into it as they walk, causing their movements to be slower than normal.

4

A popular choice with builders, this block has a blast resistance of 30, which is the same as cobblestone. However, it looks much more attractive.

5

This block is handy for making traps, as it deals fire damage. It's useless in the Nether, though, as the native mobs are immune to fire damage.

6

You can use this substance to craft several useful redstone items. It can also be combined to make several kinds of decorative blocks.

THE WITHER

Do you have the guts to take on the terrifying wither?
While you think about that, let me share some of my pro tips with you.

Finish building the wither to bring it to life, then complete the recipes to help you defeat it.

POTION OF STRENGTH

Drink a potion of strength and you'll be able to do more damage to the wither with your sword.

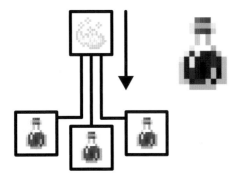

POTION OF STRENGTH RECIPE

POTION OF HEALING

A potion of healing helps you to heal. It will also harm the wither if you brew it into a splash potion.

POTION OF HEALING RECIPE

SNOW GOLEM

A snow golem will distract the wither with its snowballs, giving you the chance to get some hits in. You can make a snow golem by placing a pumpkin on top of 2 blocks of snow.

NETHER STAR

The wither drops a Nether star when defeated. This rare item can be used to craft a beacon—a structure that provides helpful status effects when you're near it.

BEACON RECIPE

FOLLOW THE EYES

If you're as keen to visit the End dimension as I am, you'll need to find an End portal. They're hidden deep underground in strongholds, and you can find them by throwing eyes of ender.

Finish the eye of ender recipe using your stickers, then follow the coordinates to find the stronghold.

DESERT

START

SAVANNA

EYE OF ENDER

When thrown, an eye of ender will travel a short distance toward the nearest stronghold. Keep throwing them until they stop traveling and land on the same spot, then dig down to find the stronghold.

EYE OF ENDER RECIPE

EXTREME HILLS

INSTRUCTIONS

East 3
South 4
East 6
South 5
East 8
North 5
West 4
North 4
East 2
North 2
West 8
South 2

FOREST

Which biome did you end up in?
Write your answer here.

_____

SURVIVAL
WITH BEAR

THE STRONGHOLD

The stronghold is a maze of corridors, and danger could be lurking around every corner. This is the perfect opportunity to work on your survival skills.

Find a path to the portal room, avoiding hostile mobs and lava and picking up loot along the way.

ENCHANTED BOOK

PAPER

START

BREAD

REDSTONE

FINISH

IRON INGOT

APPLE

19

PORTAL ROOM

Oh gosh, you've finally reached the portal! This is so exciting! Burny lava is my favorite, and you're about to cross over to the End dimension! Yay!

You'll need to activate the End portal by filling the empty frames with eyes of ender. Add a sticker of a silverfish to the info card to learn all about it.

SILVERFISH

⚔ HOSTILITY	6	❤ HEALTH	8
⚔ ATTACK	1	XP	5
DROPS		NOTHING	

ℹ Silverfish are so small that they'll sink into soul sand and suffocate.

THE END

You've finally made it to the End's main island. There's not much on the island except for endermen and the dreaded ender dragon.

It's time to make a plan – build an emergency shelter to keep you safe while you decide on your next move, and add some endermen to the scene.

PODIUM

There's a strange podium in the middle of the island, made from bedrock. The dragon seems to be very protective of it. . . .

DRAGON FIGHT

You'll need nerves of steel to defeat the ender dragon.
I'm just the person to help you win the fiercest battle of your life.

Add yourself into the scene, then complete the info boxes with the correct stickers to learn how to defeat Minecraft's deadliest boss mob.

DRAGON EGG

The dragon egg is a trophy that appears on the podium when you defeat the ender dragon. It can't be mined with a tool – you'll need to use a piston to push it onto a solid block before you can collect it.

BED

Beds explode if you try to use them in the End, which means they can be used as weapons against the dragon. Be careful you don't blow yourself up too, though!

BED RECIPE

GLASS BOTTLE

You'll need glass bottles to collect dragon's breath before you finish it off. It's a valuable substance that can be used to make lingering potions.

3

GLASS BOTTLES RECIPE

THE END CITY

You may have defeated the dragon, but that doesn't mean you can relax. If you travel to an End city on the outer islands, you'll need to be very careful.

Find stickers for each of the things you'll see in an End city, and learn more about them.

END SHIP

These floating ships are where you'll find elytra—wings that allow you to glide in Survival mode. There's also a dragon head at the end of the ship—this is the only place you'll find one.

DRAGON HEAD

ELYTRA

CHORUS FRUIT

CHORUS PLANT

These towering purple structures are the only plants that grow on the outer islands. They drop chorus fruit when mined, which can be eaten or cooked to make popped chorus fruit.

TOWER

The city is made up of several towers built from end stone and purpur blocks. You'll find hostile creatures called shulkers living inside these towers, so be very careful.

SHULKER

HOSTILITY	7	HEALTH	30
ATTACK	4	XP	5
DROPS			

Shulkers guard the End cities and shoot guided projectiles at their targets.

SHULKER SKIRMISH

Exploring the End city, you spot a shulker.
You've heard about these creatures, but you've never faced one before.

Find some stickers on your sticker sheet to complete the story of your skirmish with the shulker.

COMBAT
WITH SCOUT

You're not sure whether the creature is alive. Then it

opens its shell and you see a _____ inside. Before you

know what's happening, it shoots a _____ right at you.

You manage to hit it with your _____ and the projectile

is destroyed. But then the shulker shoots another

_____ at you. You try to deflect it with your

but you're not quick enough and it hits you. You begin to

float up into the air. You search your inventory for

something to stop it, and find a   . You're not sure

whether it will work, but you drink the   anyway.

To your relief, you stop floating upward. You're only a

little way above the ground, so you don't take much

damage when you fall back to earth. You land right next

to the shulker and hit it with your   . Defeated, it

falls over and drops a   . You're not quite sure

what this strange object does, but it better be good!

HOME, SWEET HOME

Congratulations—you've conquered all three of Minecraft's dimensions! Now you can travel back and forth to explore whenever you like.

Use stickers to build a base on the main island so you'll always have a safe place to come back to.

EXPLORING
WITH MONTY

ELYTRA ACE

Since you are the proud owner of a shiny new set of elytra, survival in all dimensions just got a lot easier. The hostile mobs will never catch you now.

Add Steve to the scene as he demonstrates how to use the elytra.

SURVIVAL
WITH BEAR

ANSWERS

Pages 6–7:

Pages 12–13:

1. Netherrack
2. Glowstone dust
3. Soul sand
4. Nether brick
5. Magma block
6. Nether quartz

Pages 16–17:

Desert

Pages 18–19: